U0690769

纳西族三大史诗英译丛书

2016年国家社会科学基金项目成果（《纳西族东巴经主要典籍英译及研究》（项目批准号：16BYY034））

丛书主编　张立玉　起国庆

汉英对照

鲁般鲁饶

牛相奎　赵净修　整理

张立玉　李　明　英译

［美］H. W. Lan　审校

The Song of Migration

WUHAN UNIVERSITY PRESS
武汉大学出版社

图书在版编目(CIP)数据

鲁般鲁饶:汉英对照/牛相奎,赵净修整理;张立玉,李明英译.—武汉:武汉大学出版社,2020.7
纳西族三大史诗英译丛书/张立玉,起国庆主编
ISBN 978-7-307-21450-7

Ⅰ.鲁… Ⅱ.①牛… ②赵… ③张… ④李… Ⅲ.纳西族—史诗—中国—汉、英 Ⅳ.I222.7

中国版本图书馆 CIP 数据核字(2020)第 060738 号

责任编辑:罗晓华 邓 喆   责任校对:李孟潇   版式设计:韩闻锦

出版发行:**武汉大学出版社** (430072 武昌 珞珈山)
(电子邮箱:cbs22@whu.edu.cn 网址:www.wdp.com.cn)
印刷:武汉中远印务有限公司
开本:720×1000 1/16 印张:9.25 字数:109 千字
版次:2020 年 7 月第 1 版 2020 年 7 月第 1 次印刷
ISBN 978-7-307-21450-7 定价:30.00 元

版权所有,不得翻印;凡购我社的图书,如有质量问题,请与当地图书销售部门联系调换。

出品单位：中南民族大学南方少数民族文库翻译研究基地
云南省少数民族古籍整理出版规划办公室

纳西族三大史诗英译丛书

编 委 会

学术顾问　王宏印　李正栓

主　　编　张立玉　起国庆
副 主 编　李　明　和六花

编委会成员（按姓氏笔画排序）：
　　　　　王向松　艾　芳　龙江莉　李克忠　李　明
　　　　　杨筱奕　张立玉　和六花　依旺的　保俊萍
　　　　　起国庆　陶开祥　涂沙丽　臧军娜

"三大史诗"前言

　　纳西族是滇西北地区的一个重要的少数民族，绝大部分居住在云南省丽江市，其余分布在云南其他县市和四川盐源、盐边、木里等县。作为较早创制本民族文字"东巴"文的民族之一，纳西族人民使用这一象形文字记录下了卷帙浩繁的东巴古籍文献，仅收藏于国内外有关学术文化机构和个人手中的东巴经文献就有近 3 万册，另有散佚于民间的东巴古籍更无法计数。

　　纳西族东巴经古籍分为祭天经、祭山神经、祭祖先经、求嗣经、祭猎神经、放替身经、解禳灾难经、祭水怪猛妖经、开丧经、祭死者经、祭风经、祭短鬼经、退口舌是非经、驱瘟神经、占卜经、道场规程经、零杂经等二十四类（参见和钟华、杨世光主编《纳西族文学史》，第 81 页，四川民族出版社，1992 年），记载了大量的纳西族古典文学作品，包括神话故事、叙事长诗、天文地理、谚语歌谣等，较全面地反映了纳西族社会历史、文学艺术、哲学思想、宗教习俗、天文历法、民族关系等方面的内容，被誉为纳西族的"圣经"和纳西族古代社会的百科全书。

　　在数以万计的纳西东巴古籍中，最著名的纳西族神话史诗当属创世史诗《创世纪》、英雄史诗《黑白之战》（又名《东术战争》《董术战争》《东埃术埃》《董埃术埃》）和爱情史诗《鲁般鲁饶》，它们被合称为纳西族的三大史诗，又被誉为东巴文学中的"三颗明珠"。

《创世纪》记载于东巴经典籍祭山神龙王经、除秽经、祭风经、消灾经、开丧经、超荐经、求寿经、退口舌是非经等多部经书中，通过生动的神话故事和栩栩如生的人物形象观照出古代纳西族风俗礼仪起源、民族迁徙史、民族经济生活形态演进史，折射出纳西民族宇宙观、哲学观和审美观。《鲁般鲁饶》是一部纳西族叙事长诗，以东巴象形文字被记载于东巴古籍中，是纳西族殉情文学中最绚丽的诗篇。作为东巴经中一部重要的经书，《鲁般鲁饶》在大祭风仪式中必会被演诵。《黑白之战》是一部纳西族英雄史诗，被完整记载于纳西族东巴经籍中，根据东巴经书《东术战争》改编创作而成，直译是"东术仇斗"，即东部落与术部落的战争。《黑白之战》是丽江也是纳西族史上第一个国家艺术基金传播交流推广项目。

2008 年 3 月 1 日，国务院颁布了首批《国家珍贵古籍名录》，110 部少数民族文字古籍入选该名录，其中就包括了以《创世纪》和《东术战争》为代表的五部东巴经古籍，足见纳西族东巴史诗在少数民族古代文学体系中的重要地位。在新的社会历史条件下，对纳西族东巴经三大史诗展开英译工作，将有助于纳西族优秀传统文化在世界范围内的弘扬和传承。

2016 年 6 月中南民族大学外语学院"英汉语言对比及应用研究团队"成功获批国家社会科学基金项目"纳西族东巴经主要典籍英译及研究"，致力于将纳西族东巴经三大史诗及其蕴涵的生态文化推向世界。项目团队在前期做了大量的文献学考证和民俗学调研的工作，在此基础上几易其稿，并聘请专家进行审校才最终完成《创世纪》《鲁般鲁饶》和《黑白之战》的英译定稿工作。

由于民族典籍多以诸如刻本、稿本、拓本、抄本的书写本形式或口耳相传的口头活态形式遗留下来，且一部典籍常常存在多个语种的版本，这就需要译者查找原始文献资料、搜集整理文献和进行版本考证，并借助文献注释进行翻译。在文献学考证阶段，团队成员充分利用学校图书馆、国家图书馆以及田野调查所在地丽江市的博物馆、研究院等机构，广泛搜集国内外有关三大史诗的文献资料，并对史诗的不同版本进行了系统梳理。

在审阅了诸多三大史诗的东巴文本和汉译版本后，团队最终确定以云南民族民间文学丽江调查队搜集、翻译、整理的《创世纪》(收录入 2012 年 7 月云南出版集团公司云南教育出版社出版的《云南少数民族叙事长诗全集》下卷) 为《创世纪》英译本的汉语原文本。该版本系 1958 年 9 月由中共云南省委宣传部组织的云南民族民间文学丽江调查队在纳西族主要聚居地——丽江、宁蒗两地对纳西族文学进行发掘、整理和研究的成果。调查队将记载在经书中的《创世纪》翻译出了六个不同的底本，并根据在丽江和宁蒗搜集到的十余件口头流传材料和摩梭人口述材料，完成了《创世纪》的汉译整理工作。《鲁般鲁饶》英译本采用牛相奎、赵净修整理的《鲁般鲁饶》(收录入 2012 年 7 月云南出版集团公司云南教育出版社出版的《云南少数民族叙事长诗全集》中卷) 为汉语原文本。该版本以由东巴经师和芳、和正才、多随合三人讲述，纳西族牛相奎、赵净修翻译的三种不同译文为主要依据，同时参考了周霖、和志武、和锡典等的三种译本，以及男女对唱形式的口头流传本《开美久命金和主本余冷排》《开美久命金和朱古羽勒排》和《东巴经·祭风部·本吕孔》等原始资料整理而成。《黑白之战》英译本采用杨世光根据东巴经典籍整理撰写的英雄史诗《东术战争》(收录于《云南少数民族古典史诗全集》上卷，于 2009 年 9 月由云南出版集团公司云南教育出版社出版）为汉语原文本。

由于民族典籍大多反映了各民族相异的语言、文学、传统、宗教以及价值观体系，因而译者只有经过充分的民俗学调研才能真正履行译者责任，不偏不倚地将原语典籍中承载的民族语言文化生态因子移植到译语生态环境中去。为此，团队成员多次前往云南省丽江市古城区、玉龙纳西族自治县等地开展田野调查，体验了"三朵节"、祭祖、婚礼庆典等一些具有浓郁纳西族特色的宗教民俗和传统节庆活动，并就纳西族民族起源和迁徙的相关历史传说，纳西族风俗礼仪、宗教意识与神灵观念，三大史诗在纳西族各方言区的流传等议题，对纳西族历史文化相关研究学者，如云南省社会科学院丽江东巴文化研究院相关领导及纳西学专家等，进行了深入访谈。

上述一系列文献学考证和民俗学调研工作给团队译者提供了大量关于纳西族东巴经典籍的原语生态信息，保证了译者对于原语生态环境的高度依归，为其后在文本移植过程中保留和再现纳西族生态因子打下了基础。

三大史诗英译本在翻译过程中得到了王宏印、李正栓等典籍英译学者的鼓励，得到了云南省少数民族古籍整理出版规划办公室主任起国庆、纳西族研究员和六花，以及丽江东巴文化研究院相关学者的指导和帮助，在此一并表示感谢。

译者团队几经润色，努力在内容表达和语体风格上再现神话史诗的原作风貌和纳西族的原语生态，但由于译者水平有限，加之原文仍有一些晦涩难解之处，译文处理不当在所难免，敬请广大读者朋友批评指正，以便修订时更正。

丛书主编：张立玉　起国庆

2020 年 1 月

前　　言

　　"鲁般鲁饶"一语，系古代纳西语的音译。"鲁"的原意是未婚男青年，这里泛指男女青年，"鲁"的去声字为放牧之意；"般"表示迁徙；"饶"表示由高处或上方（一般以西方、北方为上方）下来。"鲁般鲁饶"即"牧儿牧女迁徙下来"，可简译作"迁徙之歌"。和志武考证了《鲁般鲁饶》的产生年代，认为其产生于唐代初年，形成和发展于唐、宋两个朝代，反映了在纳西族奴隶社会中牧奴们只能通过殉情来争取自由和幸福的悲剧性主题。《鲁般鲁饶》通过纳西族奴隶社会中牧奴和牧主的矛盾，通过两种对立的理想、意志和实践准则之间的冲突来表现其"将人生有价值的东西毁灭给人看"的悲剧意识，从而揭露假、丑、恶，引起人们对真、善、美的追求。《鲁般鲁饶》讲述了男女主人公朱古羽勒排和开美久命金的爱情悲剧，与创世史诗《创世纪》和英雄史诗《黑白之战》并称为纳西族古代文学的"三颗明珠"。

　　《鲁般鲁饶》在历史上存在一些重要的东巴文文本和汉译文本。东巴文文本由各个大东巴所书写，不同的东巴书写本间略有差异。东巴文与汉译文兼有的译注本有由杨树兴、和云彩诵经，由和发源翻译的《鲁般鲁饶·祭风》，出版于20世纪80年代；以及出版于21世纪初的由和即贵诵经，由和宝林翻译的《大祭风·鲁般鲁饶》。汉译本有云南民族民间文学丽江调查队编写的《鲁般鲁饶》、和志武先生的译本《鲁般

1

鲁饶》、赵银棠先生的诗体《鲁般鲁饶》、周霖先生翻译整理的《鲁般鲁饶》、和锡典先生的译本《鲁般鲁饶》、牛向奎先生和赵净修先生整理的《鲁般鲁饶》和杨世光先生整理的散文体《朱古羽勒排与开美久命金》等版本。在审阅了诸多《鲁般鲁饶》汉译版本后，团队确定采用牛相奎、赵净修整理的《鲁般鲁饶》(收录入 2012 年 7 月云南出版集团公司云南教育出版社出版的《云南少数民族叙事长诗全集》中卷)为汉语原文本。

诚然，纳西族爱情史诗《鲁般鲁饶》在语言、结构等艺术形式层面都极具纳西族民族特色，要在英译本中完全再现《鲁般鲁饶》原文本所包含的纳西族生态语境，保留其作为纳西族爱情史诗的独特文学艺术生态，绝非易事。赋、比、兴手法的大量应用，增强了《鲁般鲁饶》的抒情性，使之具有音乐的情绪化的节奏；汉语诗歌音律特色与纳西族语言特色结合的音韵，既体现了民间诗词自由古朴的美，也表现了格律诗整齐的美。译者采用直译、意译、音译、释译、转换等方法，尽可能将颇具民族特色的语言原汁原味地移植到英译本中，力图再现这些修辞手法体现的文学效果。

由于译者团队水平有限，译文处理不当在所难免，敬请广大读者朋友批评指正，以便修订时更正。

译者：张立玉　李明

2019 年 7 月

目　录

Contents

第一章 抗 命

青青高山上，
有个放牧场。
牧儿吹竹笛，
牧女弹口弦①。

牧儿九十个，
搭着帐篷住。
牧女七十个，
围着篱栅住。

白天同放牧，
牧儿相亲如兄弟；
夜晚同歇宿，
牧女相敬如姐妹。

---

① 口弦：又称口琴，由竹篾制成，是云南纳西族人民最喜爱的
民间乐器。《南诏野史》中曾有"男吹芦笙，女奏口琴"的记载。自
古以来，纳西族就有通过演奏口琴来倾诉爱意的习俗。

Chapter 1   Disobeying the Parents

On a green mountain,

There was a grazing pasture.

The young shepherds were playing bamboo flutes,

With the young shepherdesses playing harmonicas.①

There were ninety shepherds,

Who lived in the tents they put up.

There were seventy shepherdesses,

Who lived around the hedged fences they built.

In daytime, the shepherds pastured together,

And they were as close as brothers.

At night, the shepherdesses slept together,

And they were as close as sisters.

---

① Harmonica: Harmonica, also known as oral strings, made of bamboo strips, is the most popular folk musical instrument among the Naxi people in Yunnan province. There is a historical record in *The Unofficial History of Nanzhao* telling that "men played lusheng (a folk musical instrument popular in south-west area in China) and women played harmonica". Since ancient times, the Naxi young men and women have been playing harmonicas to tell their love for each other.

九十个小伙，
哪个最能干？
朱古羽勒排①，
数他最能干。

七十个姑娘，
哪个顶灵巧？
开美久命金②，
数她顶灵巧。

小哥羽勒排，
小妹久命金，
磨盖合磨心，
两个心合心。

泉水绕青松，
久命绕着羽排。
青草围灵芝，
羽排围着久命③。

---

① 朱古羽勒排：男主人公的全名。"朱古"是姓，"羽勒排"是名。朱古羽勒排就是朱古家的羽勒排，可以简称为"羽排"。

② 开美久命金：女主人公的全名。"开美"是姓，"久命"是名，"金"意指家中独女。

③ 此处是一个比喻，暗示羽排和久命是一对佳偶。

Among the ninety young men,

Who was the ablest?

Zhugu Yulepai①

Was the ablest of all.

Among the seventy young women,

Who was the most dexterous?

Kaimei Jiuming Jin②

Was the most dexterous of all.

Brother Yulepai

And sister Jiuming Jin,

Like a pair of millstones,

Were closely attached to each other.

Like the spring water running around pine trees,

Jiuming was around brother Yupai.

Like the green grass growing around

The lingzhi mushrooms,

Yupai was around Jiuming.③

---

① Zhugu Yulepai: It is the full name of the hero. "Zhugu" is his family name and "Yulepai" is his first name. Zhugu Yulepai refers to Yulepai in Zhugu's family, and he can be called "Yupai" for short.

② Kaimei Jiuming Jin: It is the full name of the heroine. "Kaimei" is her family name and "Jiuming" is her first name. "Jin" means Jiuming is the only daughter in her family.

③ This is a metaphor to indicate that Yupai and Jiuming could be a good match for marriage.

雁有领头雁，
羊有领头羊。
小伙九十个，
羽勒排是领头雁。
姑娘七十个，
久命金是领头羊。

母羊咩咩叫，
小羊蹦蹦跳。
牧儿和牧女，
欢乐又和睦。

春天三个月，
草嫩泉水甜。
羊儿恋嫩草，
牧儿牧女心儿甜。

夏天三个月，
风吹阵阵热。
草旺羊儿肥，
牧儿牧女心儿热。

秋天三个月，
树梢见黄叶。
秋雨冷凄凄，
牧儿牧女披毡湿。

Like wild geese that had a bellwether

Or sheep that had a bellwether,

The ninety young men

Had Yulepai as their bellwether,

And the seventy young women

Had Jiuming Jin as their bellwether.

While the ewes were bleating and

the lambs jumping,

the shepherds and shepherdesses

lived happily and peacefully.

During the three months of spring,

the grass was tender and spring water was sweet.

The shepherds and shepherdesses were happy

to see the sheep enjoying the tender grass.

During the three months of summer,

the wind was blowing waves of heat.

It warmed their hearts

to see the lush grass and fat sheep.

During the three months of autumn,

leaves on tree tops turned yellow.

The chilly autumn rain

dampened the shepherds'

and shepherdesses' woolen throws.

冬天三个月，
雪山雪花飞。
羊儿嚼枯草，
牧儿牧女围火堆。

花无百日红，
草无千日鲜。
日日守旧窝，
牧场不兴旺。

树大要分枝，
儿大要自立。
小伙要迁徙，
姑娘要迁徙。

山外更有山，
天外更有天。
迁徙去远方，
去找好地方。

牧儿拔篷帐，
牧女整行装。
高山挡不住，
白鹤孔雀要远翔。

During the three months of winter,
snowflakes were whirling in the mountains.
The sheep chewed on withered grass,
and the shepherds and shepherdesses gathered
around the fire.

Just like flowers couldn't be in full bloom forever,
grass couldn't be fresh forever.
Staying on the same pastureland all the time
was not good for farming.

Trees must branch out when they became bigger,
and children must become independent
when they grew older.
The young men and young women
needed to migrate.

There were mountains beyond mountains,
and heavens beyond heavens.
Move far away,
to find more fertile land.

The young shepherds were taking down the tents,
and the young shepherdesses had started packing.
If white cranes and peacocks wanted to fly afar,
high mountains could not stop them.

父母听消息，
心急如火焚。
家家带口信，
带到牧场里。
劝说再劝说，
叮咛又叮咛。

"牧儿牧女呵，
父母的心肝，
不能迁徙呀，
不能去远方，
父母的话是金子，
快回家里来。
天上有星路，
快从星路来。
地上有草路，
快从草路来。
山上有树路，
快从树路来。
箐谷有水路，
快从水路来！"

牧儿牧女带口信，
羽排久命带口信，
口信带到家，
回话爹和妈。

But, when their parents heard the news,
They were burning with anxiety.
They sent messages to the pastureland,
They tried to dissuade them from migrating,
And they tried to exhort them to stay put.

"Ah, young shepherds and shepherdesses,
You are the nearest and dearest to our heart,
So you cannot migrate and cannot go afar.
Parents' words are gold,
So come home quickly.
There is the milky way in the sky,
Come back by it quickly.
There are grass roads on the ground,
Come back quickly through those roads.
There are forest paths in the mountains,
Come back quickly by those paths.
There are waterways through the valleys,
Come back quickly across them!"

The shepherds and shepherdesses
With Yupai and Jiuming,
Sent the messages back home,
Replying to their fathers and mothers:

"天上有星路①，
三星带星路。
三星一出来，
星宿满天闪。
天上星路走不成，
牧儿牧女不能来。

"地上有草路，
蒿草带草路。
蒿草一露头，
青草遍地长。
地上草路走不成，
牧儿牧女不能来。

"山上有树路，
杜鹃带树路。
杜鹃花一开，
树木满山岗。
山上树路走不成，
牧儿牧女不能来。

---

① 星路：在一些东巴经典籍如《创世纪》中，星路、草路、树路、水路指迁徙的必经之路。此处，星路、草路、树路、水路指牧儿牧女归家的必经之路。

"There is indeed the milky way① in the sky,

led by Triangulum. But,

once Triangulum comes out,

the constellation of stars will sparkle all over the sky.

The milky way cannot be passed,

your young shepherds and shepherdesses cannot come back.

"There are indeed grass roads on the ground,

led by the wormwood. But,

once the wormwood appears,

the green grass will spread everywhere.

The grass roads cannot be passed,

and your young shepherds and shepherdesses

cannot come back.

"There are indeed forest paths in the mountains,

led by the azaleas. But,

once the azaleas bloom,

The hillocks will be clad with trees.

The forest paths cannot be passed,

and your young shepherds and shepherdesses cannot come

back.

----

① The milky way: In some Dongba classics, like in *The Creation of the World*, the milky way, the grass roads, the forest paths and the waterways refer to the ways which must be passed for migration. Here, the four paths refer to the ways which have to be passed for young shepherds and shepherdesses to go home.

"菁谷有水路，
蛟龙带水路。
龙带洪水来，
大水满菁淌。
菁谷水路走不成，
牧儿牧女不能来。"

远看好地方，
真个好风光。
山泉清亮亮，
山花红又香。
树林绿莹莹，
草滩翠汪汪。
牧儿牧女呵，
心里多喜欢。

竹笛声悠悠，
飘过千重山。
口弦声铮铮，
越过万重冈。

牧群要远走，
越远越有好风光。
牧儿牧女呵，
不愿往回转。

"There are indeed waterways through the valleys,

led by the flood dragon.

But when the dragon comes with the flood,

the valleys will be filled with water.

The waterways cannot be passed,

And your young shepherds and shepherdesses cannot come

back.

Looking at the place far away,

they enjoyed a breathtaking view of the mountains:

the clear and bright springs,

the red and sweet flowers,

the glossy and green woods, and

the bluish green grass.

Ah, the young shepherds and shepherdesses

were full of joy in their heart.

Floating through thousands of hills

was the melodious sound of the bamboo flutes.

Crossing thousands of hillocks

was the reedy sound of the harmonicas.

The herd was to travel far away because,

the farther away, the more wonderful the sight.

Ah, the young shepherds and shepherdesses

did not want to take the road back.

等了七个月，
只见白云飘，
不见人回来，
父母心更焦！

等了九个月，
只见清泉流，
不见人回来，
父母心更愁！

家里又带信，
带到牧场里。
传话给儿女，
劝说又叮咛：

"古树寿岁长，
愿把树寿给鲜花。
大河寿岁长，
愿把河寿给浪花。
老人寿岁长，
愿把寿岁给青年。
牧儿牧女们，
赶快回家来！"

羽排小哥捎家信，
久命小妹带口信，
牧儿牧女们，
约齐把话回。

Seven months of waiting
brought but the clouds floating.
Without seeing the children returning,
the parents became even more anxious!

Nine months of waiting
brought but the clear spring flowing.
Without seeing the children returning,
the parents became even more worried!

Each family sent another message
to the grazing land,
to their sons and daughters,
urging and exhorting:

"Big trees with long lives
are willing to devote their longevity to flowers.
Great rivers with long lives
are willing to devote their longevity to waves.
Elderly people with long lives
are willing to devote their longevity to their youngsters.
Young shepherds and shepherdesses,
come home quickly!"

Brother Yulepai sent his message,
so did sister Jiuming Jin.
The young shepherds and shepherdesses
sent their message together:

"鲜花会凋谢，
树寿不能接给它，
浪花会消逝，
河寿不能接给它。
青春去不回，
人们怎能留住它？

"古树老枝遮日光，
小树弱蔫蔫。
浊流壅塞河道上，
清水难流畅。
栅栏关马马不壮，
儿女在家不自在！

"树林绿葱葱，
鲜花最美丽。
河水清汪汪，
浪花最美丽。
人生在世上，
青春最美丽。

"一天里，
不会有两次早晨。
一个年头里，
不会有两度新春。
雏鹰长壮了，
要趁时远飞。
儿女长大了，
要自由迁徙！"

"Flowers will wither,
even being endowed with the longevity of big trees;
Waves will disappear,
even being endowed with the longevity of great rivers;
Youth will pass without returning,
and how could people put a hold on it?

"Branches of big trees shade the sunshine,
causing the little trees to weaken and fade.
Muddy streams block the river course,
impeding the flowing of the clear river.
Just as horses locked up by fences cannot be strong,
children locked up at home cannot grow up!

"Though the woods are lush and green,
fresh flowers are the most beautiful.
Though the rivers are vast and deep,
waves are the most beautiful.
When humans live in this world,
the youth in his life is the most beautiful.

"In one day,
there cannot be two mornings.
In one year,
there cannot be two springs.
When baby eagles become strong,
they should fly far away when they can.
When children grow up,
they should migrate with the freedom they have!"

父亲急呵急，
母亲愁呵愁。
白鹤云中飞，
请它去接儿女们。
白鹤高声叫，
叫得山巅聚白云，
白云变白雪，
不能接回青年们。

布谷来回飞，
请它去接儿女们。
布谷声声叫：
"有早没有晚，"
忙着要寻食，
不能接回青年们。

蝉鸣树梢头，
请它去接儿女们。
蝉儿叫嚷嚷，
冬天还未到，
蝉壳就蜕了，
不能接回青年们。

野鸭水上飞，
请它去接儿女们。
野鸭嘎嘎叫，
叫来滂沱雨，
雨打翅膀难远飞，
不能接回青年们。

Fathers became more and more anxious, while
mothers became more and more worried.
The white crane that was flying in the clouds
was asked to bring the children back.
The crane cried with such a powerful voice,
that it gathered white clouds on the mountain tops.
But the white clouds turned into white snow,
and the youngsters were not brought back.

The cuckoo that was flying homeward
was asked to bring the children back.
But the cuckoo shouted again and again:
"My work has a beginning but not an end."
Busy with foraging for food,
it could not bring the youngsters back.

The cicada that was chirping on the treetop
was asked to bring the children back.
But screeching over and over,
the cicada would shell its husk
before winter came.
It could not bring the youngsters back.

The wild duck that was flying over the water
was asked to bring the children back.
But quacking again and again,
the duck called forth the torrential rain,
which hit the duck's wings too hard for it to fly away.
The duck could not bring the youngsters back.

麂子林中跑，
请它去接儿女们。
母麂住松林，
小麂住栗林，
麂子居住在两处，
不能接回青年们。

羚羊岩间跳，
请它去接儿女们。
母羊住高崖，
小羊住低崖，
羚羊居住在两处，
不能接回青年们。

鱼儿水里游，
请它去接儿女们。
大鱼游大潭，
小鱼游小潭，
大鱼小鱼分开游，
不能接回青年们。

坡头绶带鸟①，
请它去接儿女们。

———————

① 绶带鸟：一般指中国绶带鸟。这是生活在中国云南南部的一种鸟类，又被称作亚洲绶带鸟。它中等大小，有两种颜色，有一个闪亮的黑色头部和突出的羽冠。绶带鸟的雌雄很容易被区分，雄性绶带鸟尾部中间有两条长达 25 厘米的中央尾羽。

The muntjacs that were running in the woods
were asked to bring the children back.
But the mother muntjac was living in the pine wood,
while the baby muntjac, in the chestnut wood.
Living far away from each other,
the muntjacs could not bring the youngsters back.

The antelopes that were skipping among the rocks
were asked to bring the children back.
But the mother antelope lived among the high rocks,
while the baby antelope, among the low ones.
Living far away from each other,
the antelopes could not bring the youngsters back.

The fishes swimming in the water
were asked to bring the children back.
But the big fishes was swimming in the deep pool,
while the small fishes, in the shallow one.
Swimming separately from each other,
the fishes could not bring the youngsters back.

The paradise flycatcher① that was staying by the slope
was asked to bring the children back.

---

① The paradise flycatcher: It is a kind of bird living in southern Yunnan, China, which is also called Asian paradise flycatcher. It is of medium size, of two colour types, with a shiny black head and prominent crown plumage. The male is easily distinguished, with a pair of central tail feathers elongated at the back, up to 25cm.

绶带尾巴长，
雄鸟不带儿，
雌鸟要喂儿，
不能接回青年们。

塘边小青蛙，
请它去接儿女们。
青蛙四脚只顾蹦，
会跳不会走，
有嘴没有舌，
不能接回青年们。

崖上小燕子，
请它去接儿女们。
燕子尾巴分两岔，
飞东又飞西，
成天筑窝忙，
不能接回青年们。

河边鹡鸰鸟，
请它去接儿女们。
鹡鸰白头顶，
点头又点尾，
徘徊河边不起身，
不能接回青年们。

But the long-tailed flycatcher,

with her male partner not helping to raise the babies,

had to feed them by herself.

The flycatcher could not bring the youngsters back.

The little frog that was living in the pond

was asked to bring the children back.

But with its four feet jumping,

the frog could leap but not walk.

And with its tongueless mouth,

it could not bring the youngsters back.

The little swallow that was dashing around the cliff

was asked to bring the children back.

But with its scissor-blade tails,

it flew east and west.

Busy with building the nest,

it could not bring the youngsters back.

The wagtail that was by the river

was asked to bring the children back.

But with its white head

and its tail wagging,

it paced by the riverbank and would not take off.

The wagtail could not bring the youngsters back.

花雕晴空飞，
请它去接儿女们。
花雕高空三盘旋，
低空三盘旋，
不愿歇到地上来，
不能接回青年们。

父母着急了，
坡头筑起白石墙。
白墙有九道，
不让牧儿朝外跑。

父母心慌了，
山腰筑起黑石墙。
黑墙有七堵，
不让牧女往外跑。

The sparrow hawk that was soaring in the clear sky
was asked to bring the children back.
It glided around in the high sky,
then glided around in the low sky,
but it would not land on the ground.
It could not bring the youngsters back.

Becoming very distressed,
the parents built white stone walls along the mountain ridges.
Nine white walls were built
to prevent the young shepherds from leaving away.

Becoming very nervous,
the parents built black stone walls on the mountainsides.
Seven black walls were built
to prevent the young shepherdesses from leaving away.

第二章 妆 饰

草坪绿茵茵，
飞来片片云。
不是云片片呵，
那是羊儿群。

牧歌声阵阵，
羊儿声咩咩。
竹笛声悠悠，
口弦声铮铮。

羽排小哥拆松枝，
吆羊慢腾腾。
久命小妹拆柳条，
赶羊慢吞吞。

牧儿要迁徙，
打扮要英俊。
牧女想送几件礼，
礼物难找寻。

Chapter 2　Preparing for the Journey

Over the green and lush grazing land
floated pieces of clouds.
But, no, they were not clouds,
only flocks of sheep.

Pastoral songs wafted in the air, mingled with
the bleating of sheep everywhere.
The sound of the bamboo flutes lingered on, mingled with
the harmonicas' reedy melodies.

Little brother Yupai broke a small branch off a pine tree,
tending the sheep leisurely.
Little sister Jiuming broke a small branch off a willow tree,
herding the sheep calmly.

To migrate, the shepherds
should dress handsomely.
But it was too hard for the shepherdesses
to prepare gratified gifts.

牧女要迁徙，
打扮要美丽。
牧儿想送几件礼，
礼品凑不齐。

哪里有珍珠？
哪里有金银？
羽排低头闷闷想，
久命走走又停停。
徘徊心不定，
忘了顾羊群。

口哨声悠悠，
羊群聚拢来。
九羊九个名，
九羊九张脸。
点来又点去，
少了一只羊。

一只白额羊，
不知去哪里。
丢羊不去找，
牧神会生气。

羽排丢了羊，
兄弟都去找。
久命丢了羊，
姐妹都去找。

To migrate, the shepherdesses
would like to dress beautifully.
But it was too hard for the shepherds
to prepare gratified gifts.

Where to find pearls?
Where to find gold and silver?
Yupai lowered his head thinking moodily,
While Jiuming was walking absent-mindedly.
Wandering with so much on their minds,
they forgot about their flocks of sheep.

When the whistle sounded slowly,
the flocks gathered together.
Nine sheep all had their names, and
nine sheep all had their appearances.
After counting the sheep again and again,
they found that there was one sheep lost.

It was the one with the white-forehead:
Where could it be going?
If they were not to find it,
they would anger the god of animal husbandry.

When Yupai lost a sheep,
all brothers went on the search for it.
When Jiuming lost a sheep,
all sisters went on the search for it.

翻过九重山，
不见羊的影。
穿过九片林，
忽闻羊叫声。

顺声往前找，
来到山崖边。
有棵大神树，
撑天立云间。
枝是珊瑚枝，
叶是碧玉叶，
开的金花和银花，
结的珍珠和宝石。
乖乖白额羊，
树下啃玉叶。

冬天三个月，
北风扫残叶。
大雪压枝头，
神树不落叶。

夏天三个月，
大雨浇滂沱。
哗哗打神树，
神树不掉果。

Having climbed nine mountains,
they still had no sight of the sheep.
But after walking across nine woods,
they suddenly heard the bleating of sheep.

Following the sound,
they came to the edge of a cliff:
There was a big sacred tree,
standing high into the clouds,
with coral branches
and jade leaves.
It bloomed gold and silver flowers,
yielding fruits of pearls and jewels.
The gentle white-forehead sheep
was grazing on the jade leaves under the tree.

In the three months of winter,
with the north wind clearing away the falling leaves
and the heavy snow pressing the branch tips,
the sacred tree didn't shed a leaf.

In the three months of summer,
with the heavy rain coming down in sheets
hitting the sacred tree,
the tree didn't drop a fruit.

碧玉亮莹莹，
难迷小伙心。
稀罕神树呀，
迷了小伙心。

珍珠亮晶晶，
难迷姑娘心。
稀奇神树呀，
迷了姑娘心。

牧儿牧女高兴了，
高高兴兴来商量。
摘下果子当食粮，
扯下叶子来喂羊，
折下枝桠搭羊栏。

树梢栖黑鹰，
鹰会来乱叼。
抽下细马尾，
做个扣子下黑鹰，
不让黑鹰来捣闹。

树腰栖马蜂，
马蜂会来蜇。
松明扎火把，
点火燎蜂窝，
不让马蜂来作恶。

Though jade was sparkling bright,
its charm could hardly dazzle the young men.
But the rare and sacred tree,
it fascinated them.

Though pearls were glittering bright,
their glitter could hardly dazzle the young women.
But the rare and sacred tree,
it fascinated them.

The young shepherds and shepherdesses were delighted,
talking with each other joyfully:
Let's pick off the fruits for us to eat,
pull up the leaves for the sheep to feed on,
and break off the twigs to build the pens
for the sheep to stay in.

But the black hawk perching on the tree top
could swoop down any time.
The thin horsetail hair was used
to make a ring to keep the hawk away,
preventing it from doing harm.

On the tree trunk was a hornet,
and it could sting any time.
The pine twigs were used
to scorch the hornet's nest,
not letting it do evil.

树下歇老虎，
虎恶会扑咬。
烧竹放炸炮，
把虎撵跑了，
不愁老虎来袭扰。

白鹤飞来了，
锦鸡飞来了，
马鹿跑来了，
羚羊跑来了。
珍禽飞呵飞，
异兽跳呵跳，
牧儿多欢乐，
牧女齐欢笑。

日被月送走，
月被年送走。
时光像支箭，
一去不回头。

才像过一时，
却是三时了。
才像过一天，
却是三天了。
才像过一月，
却是三月了。

Under the tree a tiger was resting,

but it could attack people any time.

The bamboos were burned with crackling noises

to scare the tiger away,

setting everyone free from the harassment of the tiger.

Then the white crane came, flying,

so did the golden pheasant.

The red deer came, running,

so did the antelope.

Exotic birds were flying.

Exotic animals were jumping.

The young shepherds were full of joy,

and the young shepherdesses were laughing together.

The day turned into the month,

and the month, into the year.

Time was like an arrow,

flying by and never returning.

It felt like one hour had just passed,

but three had actually gone by.

It felt like a day had just passed,

but three had actually gone by.

It felt like one month had just passed,

but three had actually gone by.

好男挂宝刀，
挂上宝刀才英俊。
好女戴首饰，
戴上首饰才美丽。

挖开黄土找黄金，
掘开白土找白银，
玛瑙珍珠到处有，
牧儿牧女仔细寻。

久命拿镰刀，
羽排拿斧子。
斧子劈金树，
砍刀砍银枝。

斧子不锐利，
砍树树无痕。
砍刀不锋利，
砍枝枝无痕。

只好又转回，
重新制刀斧。
三张铁犁铧①，
拿来打刀斧。

---

① 犁铧：耕地时安装在犁上，用来破土的铁片。

A young man would like to wear a treasured sword,

because he looked handsome with it.

A young lady would like to wear jewelry,

because she looked pretty with it.

Loess was dug for gold.

Clay was dug for silver.

Pearls and agates were everywhere.

The young shepherds and shepherdesses just had to search

for them carefully.

Jiuming was holding a cutting sickle,

while Yupai, a hacking axe.

The axe was for chopping the gold tree,

while the sickle, the silver branches.

But the axe was too dull

to leave any mark on the tree.

The sickle was not sharp enough

to leave any trace on the branches.

They had no choice but

to remake the sickle and the axe.

Three iron plowshares①

were used to remake the sickle and the axe.

---

① Plowshare: A part of a plow that cuts the furrow and is made of
metal.

剥了花马皮，
拿来做风箱。
砍来青栗树，
烧成好木炭。

不会制刀斧，
去请铁匠来。
杀牛做早饭，
杀猪做午饭，
杀羊做晚饭。

刀斧打出来，
还有淬淬火。
请来白尾龙，
龙吐神水来淬火，
新刀坚硬不会弯，
新斧坚硬能剁锅。

刀斧淬了火，
要安刀斧把。
去请独角兽，
兽角来做刀斧把。

新斧石上磨，
斧头锐利了。
新刀石上磨，
刀口锋利了。

The horse was skinned
to make the bellows.
The green chestnut tree was cut
to be burned into fine charcoal.

Not knowing how to make the sickle and axe,
they invited a blacksmith for
butchering a cow to make breakfast,
a pig for lunch,
and a sheep for dinner.

The sickle and axe were forged,
and they then needed to be quenched.
A white-tailed dragon was invited
to spit the mystery water:
The new sickle would be strong and not bend,
and the new axe would be strong and could chop up pots.

After being quenched,
the sickle and axe were ready for their handles.
A unicorn was invited,
to make the handles with its horn.

After being ground on the stone,
the axe's edge was sharp.
After being ground on the stone,
the sickle's blade was sharp.

羽排和久命，
来把神树砍。
用力砍一下，
砍飞白银片，
落在白石山。

白银没人打，
请个银匠来。
打成银手镯，
打成银耳环。

姑娘戴上银耳环，
耳环响叮叮。
小伙看姑娘，
姑娘多美丽。

小伙戴银镯，
银镯亮闪闪。
姑娘看小伙，
小伙多漂亮。

久命和羽排，
又砍神树干。
用力砍一下，
砍飞黄金片，
落在黄土山。

Yupai and Jiuming then
came to cut the sacred tree.
With one strike,
they sent pieces of silver into the air
and then onto the white stone mountain.

To mould the silver,
they invited a silversmith for
casting silver bracelets,
casting silver earrings.

The young women put on the silver earrings,
jingling and clattering.
The young men gazed adoringly at the young women,
who looked so beautiful.

The young men put on the silver bracelets,
sparkling and glittering.
The young women gazed adoringly at the young men,
who looked so handsome.

Jiuming and Yupai then
came to cut the trunk of the sacred tree.
With one strike,
they sent pieces of gold into the air
and then onto the loess mountain.

黄金没人打，
请个金匠来，
做成金手镯，
做成金耳环。

姑娘戴上金耳环，
耳环亮晶晶。
小伙看姑娘，
姑娘多美丽。

小伙戴金镯，
金镯亮闪闪。
姑娘看小伙，
小伙多漂亮。

羽排和久命，
又把神树砍。
用力砍一下，
砍飞绿玉片，
落在绿水潭。

碧玉没人琢，
请个玉匠来，
碧玉嵌刀鞘①，
碧玉镶耳环。

---

① 刀鞘：刀鞘指用来装刀刃的套子。玉是一种珍贵的石头，在中国文化中象征着财富、和平、高贵和纯洁。将玉器镶嵌在鞘中，可以显示主人的高贵地位。

To mould the gold,
they invited a goldsmith for
casting gold bracelets,
casting gold earrings.

The young women put on the gold earrings,
sparkling and glittering.
The young men gazed adoringly at the young women,
who looked so beautiful.

The young men put on the gold bracelets,
glistening and glittering.
The young women gazed adoringly at the young men,
who looked so handsome.

Yupai and Jiuming
came to cut the sacred tree again.
With one strike,
they sent pieces of emerald into the air
and then into the green pool.

To cut the jade,
they invited a jadesmith for
engraving the jade to decorate sheaths①,
engraving the jade to decorate earrings.

---

① Sheath: A sheath is a covering for the blade of a knife. Jade is a kind of precious stone, symbolizing wealth, peace, nobility and purity in Chinese culture. The sheaths inlaid with jade may show the high status of the host.

姑娘戴上玉耳环，
耳环晃眼睛。
小伙看姑娘，
姑娘多美丽。

小伙挂上镶玉刀，
宝刀闪闪亮。
姑娘看小伙，
小伙多漂亮。

久命和羽排，
又砍神树干。
用力砍一下，
砍飞海螺片，
落在白石海。

海螺制镜框，
姑娘戴圆镜。
小伙看姑娘，
姑娘多美丽。

海螺雕带扣，
小伙挂螺扣。
姑娘看小伙，
小伙多漂亮。

The young women put on the jade earrings,

blinking and dazzling.

The young men gazed adoringly at the young women,

who looked so beautiful.

The young men put on the sword inlaid with jade,

glittering and shining.

The young women gazed adoringly at the young men,

who looked so handsome.

Jiuming and Yupai

came to cut the sacred tree again.

With one strike,

they sent pieces of conch into the air

and then into the white stone sea.

The conch was made into spectacle frames

for the young women to wear.

The young men gazed adoringly at the young women,

who looked so beautiful.

The conch was made into belt buttons

for the young men to wear.

The young women gazed adoringly at the young men,

who looked so handsome.

羽排和久命，
又把神树砍。
用力砍一下，
砍飞珍珠串，
落在草坪上。

珍珠串项链，
姑娘戴项链。
小伙看姑娘，
姑娘多美丽。

珍珠嵌腰带，
小伙系腰带。
姑娘看小伙，
小伙多漂亮。

久命和羽排，
又砍神树干。
用力砍一下，
砍飞宝石片，
落在雪地上。

宝石串璎珞，
姑娘佩璎珞。
小伙看姑娘，
姑娘多美丽。

Yupai and Jiuming,

came to cut the sacred tree again.

With one strike,

they sent strings of pearls into the air

and then on the lawn.

The pearl necklaces

were worn by the young women.

The young men gazed adoringly at the young women,

who looked so beautiful.

The waistbands inlaid with the pearls

were worn by the young men.

The young women gazed adoringly at the young men,

who looked so handsome.

Jiuming and Yupai,

came to cut the trunk of the sacred tree again.

With one strike,

they sent pieces of gem into the air

and then on the snow.

The gem stone necklaces

were worn by the young women.

The young men gazed adoringly at the young women,

who looked so beautiful.

宝石嵌弩弓①，
小伙背弩弓。
姑娘看小伙，
小伙多漂亮。

羽排和久命，
又砍神树干。
用力砍一下，
砍飞红铜片，
落在高山上。

高山有赤虎②，
要去射赤虎。
红铜做箭镞，
羽排去射虎。

虎皮做刀鞘，
虎皮做箭袋，
虎皮做垫褥，
虎皮做衣裳。

---

① 弩弓：纳西族地区使用的一种传统武器，由一种固定在较大
木片上的弓组成，用以发射短而重的箭。

② 赤虎："赤"即红色，此处用来形容虎皮的颜色。据记录，
印支虎是一种生活在中国古代西南地区的老虎，有着深红色的皮毛。

The crossbows① inlaid with gem stones
were carried by the young men.
The young women gazed adoringly at the young men,
who looked so handsome.

Yupai and Jiuming,
came to cut the trunk of the sacred tree again.
With one strike,
they sent pieces of red copper into the air
and then onto the high mountain.

There were red tigers② in the mountain,
which was Yupai's hunting target.
With arrowheads made of the red copper,
Yupai went for hunting.

Tiger skin was used to make sheaths.
Tiger skin was used to make arrow cases.
Tiger skin was used to make mattresses.
Tiger skin was used to make clothes...

---

① Crossbow: A traditional weapon used in the Naxi areas, which consists of a bow that is fixed onto a larger piece of wood, and that shoots short heavy arrows.

② Red tiger: "Red" describes the color of the tiger skin. It is recorded that Panthera tigris ssp. Corbetti is a species of tiger which used to live in south-west region of China in ancient times. This species of tiger is featured by its dark red color.

姑娘垫虎皮，
姑娘穿皮衣。
小伙看姑娘，
姑娘多美丽。

小伙挂箭袋，
小伙挎宝剑。
姑娘看小伙，
小伙多漂亮。

坡头生黄竹，
黄竹生三丛。
黄竹无人管，
伴竹只有风。

谁来钻竹眼？
小虫来钻眼。
谁来吹竹管？
清风吹竹管。

清风吹过来，
竹管嚯嚯鸣。
一吹百个声，
一吹千个音。

The young women used the tiger skin to make mats,
and they worn tiger skin clothes.
The young men gazed adoringly at the young women,
who looked so beautiful.

The young men put on the arrow cases,
and they carried the treasured sword.
The young women gazed adoringly at the young men,
who looked so handsome.

On the slope, there grew yellow bamboos.
There were three clumps of them.
With no one taking care of the yellow bamboos,
their only companion was the wind.

Who would drill the holes on the bamboo?
Bugs would do it.
Who would play bamboo flutes?
The cool breeze would do it.

When the cool breeze blew,
the bamboo tubes began to whistle.
One blow produced a hundred kinds of sound.
One blow produced a thousand kinds of sound.

砍来黄竹管，
做成新竹笛，
做成新口弦。
竹笛送小伙，
口弦送姑娘。

迁徙礼物送齐了，
小伙英俊了，
姑娘美丽了，
个个合意了。

羽排吹起新竹笛，
叽哩叽哩响。
打动久命心，
久命好喜欢。

久命吹起新口弦，
阿喂阿喂响。
叩动羽排心，
羽排好喜欢。

Yellow bamboos were cut

to make new bamboo flutes

and new harmonicas.

Bamboo flutes were for the young men,

And harmonicas were for the young women.

All gifts had been prepared for migration.

Handsome were the young men,

and pretty were the young women.

All were ready and gratified.

Yupai played his new bamboo flute,

sounding euphoric.

Moved by the melody,

Jiuming was enamoured with it.

Jiuming played her new harmonica,

sounding pleasant.

Touched by the melody,

Yupai was enchanted with it.

第三章 迁 徙

骏马备上金子鞍，
猎犬套上银项圈。
小伙身上挂宝刀，
姑娘戴上珍珠串。

牧儿要迁徙，
牧女要迁徙，
一齐来商量，
选个好日子。

约定冬天走。
冬天三个月，
白鹤带白雪。
白雪封山岭，
白雪封树林。
冬天走不成。

Chapter 3　Migrating

The fine horses were in gold saddles,
and hound dogs wore silver collars.
The young men had put on treasured swords,
and the young women, pearl necklaces.

The young shepherds were ready to migrate,
and so were the young shepherdesses.
They gathered together
to choose an auspicious day.

The choice of winter—
during the three months of winter,
white cranes would bring white snow,
making the mountains impassable,
making the woods impassable.
Traveling in winter was impossible.

约定春天走。
春天三个月，
布谷声声催。
小草刚发青，
豆麦还未熟。
春天走不成。

约定夏天走。
夏天三个月，
大雨下不停。
洪水到处流，
泥深陷马蹄。
夏天走不成。

夏去秋又来，
秋天三个月。
山上开金花，
箐里开银花。
树上白果熟，
地里五谷熟。

秋天日子好，
秋天最宜走。
牧儿牧女们，
约定要远游。

The choice of spring—

during the three months of spring,

cuckoos would urge ceaselessly.

The little grass would be just sprouting,

and beans and wheats would not be ripe.

Traveling in spring was impossible.

The choice of summer—

during the three months of summer,

heavy rain would pour without stop,

flood water would be all over,

and the horses would be trapped deep in the mud.

Traveling in summer was impossible.

Autumn came after summer.

During the three months of autumn,

golden flowers would bloom in the mountains

and so would silver flowers in the valleys.

All fruits would ripen on the trees,

and so would the grains in the field.

Autumn was a good choice

and the most suitable.

The young shepherds and shepherdesses

agreed to move away then.

刨开九道白石墙，
小伙跑出来。
推倒九道黑石墙，
姑娘跑出来。

牧儿牧女要迁徙，
牧儿牧女要远翔，
快快乐乐一起走，
热热闹闹往前赶。

一路笑着走，
一路走着唱。
脚步快如风，
来到大河边。

小伙走得快，
早到河对岸。
姑娘走得慢，
还在河这边。

洪水泻下来，
河水上涨了。
河上小木桥，
被水冲走了。

The young shepherds took down the nine white stone walls,

and they ran away.

The young shepherdesses pushed down the nine black stone walls,

and they ran away.

Determined to migrate and

determined to fly far away,

the young shepherds and shepherdesses journeyed together delightedly.

They hurried forward chit-chatting lively.

Walking along, they were laughing all the way.

Walking along, they were singing all the way.

With steps moving as fast as the wind,

they reached the side of a large river.

The young men walked faster,

and they quickly arrived on the other side.

The young women walked more slowly,

and they were still on this side.

The flood came,

and the river rose high.

The wood bridge over the river

was washed away.

九十个小伙，
隔在河对岸。
七十个姑娘，
隔在河这边。

眼珠滴溜转，
望不见姑娘。
嗓音脆脆响，
小伙听不见。

九十个小伙，
河上搭石桥。
石桥一边搭，
石桥一边塌。

石桥没搭成，
掉了麂皮鞋。
鞋丢不心疼，
不见姑娘心儿疼。

七十个姑娘，
河上来搭桥。
搭座麻秆桥，
一踩就断了。

麻桥没搭成，
掉了麂皮鞋。
鞋丢不心疼，
不见小伙心儿疼。

The ninety young men
were on the other side.
The seventy young women
were still on this side.

The eyes were searching warily,
but they spotted no signs of the young women.
The calling was shouted clearly,
but it could not be heard by the young men.

The ninety young men
began to build a stone bridge over the river.
But the stone bridge was collapsing
as it was being built.

Their stone bridge could not be built,
and they also lost their the chamois leather shoes.
Yet they worried not about their lost shoes,
but about not seeing the young women.

The seventy young women
began to build a bridge over the river.
The bridge was made of hemp stalk,
but it was broken when stepped on.

Their hemp stalk bridge failed,
and they also lost their chamois leather shoes.
Yet they worried not about their lost shoes,
but about not seeing the young men.

羽排主意多，
找拢牧儿来商量。
松木做小船，
柏木做船桨。

左边划三下，
右边划三下，
划到对岸了，
不怕河水再隔了。

久命有智谋，
找拢牧女来商量。
杀只大公羊，
羊皮做革囊。

手也划三下，
脚也蹬三下，
划到对岸了，
不怕河水再隔了。

河边枯树上，
蜘蛛在结网。
不会架溜索，
跟着蜘蛛学。

藤篾做溜索，
桦木做溜斗。
溜索架起来，
不怕河水来阻隔。

The resourceful Yupai
decided together with the other young men,
to use pine wood to build small boats
and cedar wood to make quants.

Rowing three times on the left each time,
and then three times on the right,
they reached the opposite bank,
no longer afraid of being separated by the river.

The clever Jiuming
decided together with the other young women,
to butcher a big ram
to make leather bags.

Rowing three times by hand each time,
and then three times by foot,
they reached the opposite bank,
no longer afraid of being separated by the river.

On the dead tree branches by the river,
spiders were netting.
Not knowing how to build a zip line,
the young women learned from the spiders.

The vines were used to make the line,
and the birch was used to make the bucket.
The zip line was built,
and the river was no longer a barrier.

65

哥哥姐姐团聚了，
小弟小妹相会了。
欢喜莫过久命金，
高兴莫过羽勒排。

高高山尖上，
篝火烧得旺。
牧儿牧女们，
欢聚篝火旁。

鱼儿水里游，
蜜蜂花间闹。
相爱的伴侣呵，
又在一起了。

The elder brothers and sisters reunited,
and young brothers and sisters met again.
But none was happier than Jiuming,
and none was more delighted than Yupai.

On the top of the high mountain,
a campfire was blazing brightly.
The young shepherds and shepherdesses
merrily gathered around it.

Like fish swimming merrily together
and bees flirting among the flowers,
companions in love
gathered together once again.

第四章　阻　　隔

来到半路上，
干粮吃光了。
翻山又过河，
身子劳累了。

天高星岩①下，
有个岩洞窄又小。
岩洞不大去开拓，
相好人儿暂住下。

高山阳坡下，
有块平地像巴掌。
平地不大去辟宽，
相好人儿种荞麦。

荞子收上来，
吃的备下了。
麻皮织成布，
穿的备下了。

---

① 星岩：纳西族神话传说中的一座神圣的悬崖。

Chapter 4　Facing Obstacles

Half way on their journey,

they ran out of food.

Having crossed mountains and rivers,

they were worn out.

Under the Star Rock①,

was a narrow and small cave.

The cave could be expanded,

for the young lovers moved into it temporarily.

Under the sunny slope of the high mountains,

was a piece of flat land like a palm.

The land could be widened,

but the young lovers had started to plant buckwheat in.

The buckwheat was reaped,

and the food was well prepared.

The flax yarn was weaved into cloth,

and the clothings were well prepared.

---

① The Star Rock: It is a sacred cliff in the Naxi legend.

牧儿又启程，
牧女又动身，
迁徙去远方，
要找好地方。

姐姐格贞先走了，
哥哥精那先走了，
妹妹姑鸾也走了，
弟弟知由也走了，①
许多兄弟都走了，
许多姐妹都走了。
小妹开美久命金，
心事重重也走了。
小弟朱古羽勒排，
父母赶来截着了。

天穹没有走，
星星走掉了，
天和星星分开了。

地坪没有走，
青草走掉了，
地坪青草分开了。

---

① 格贞，精那，姑鸾，知由：均为牧儿和牧女的名字。

The young shepherds set out again,

and the young shepherdesses set out again.

They were determined to migrate far away,

to find good places.

Elder sister Gezhen went first.

Elder brother Jingna went first.

Younger sister Guluan left.

Younger brother Zhiyou also left.①

Many brothers set off.

Many sisters set off.

Little sister Kaimei Jiuming Jin

left with much on her mind,

because little brother Zhugu Yulepai

was held back by his parents.

The sky did not move,

but the stars did.

The sky and the stars were separated.

The terrace did not move,

but the green grass did.

The terrace and the grass were separated.

---

① Gezhen, Jingna, Guluan and Zhiyou are the names of shepherds and shepherdesses.

堤岸没有走，
清水走掉了，
水和堤岸分开了。

树木没有走，
树叶走掉了，
树和叶子分开了。

朱古羽勒排，
双眼泪涌流。
开美久命金，
一步三回头。
情郎情女分开了，
山隔水阻难相逢。

翻过九重山，
来到新地方。
过了七重水，
来到好地方。

山坡牧草旺，
坝子多宽敞，
河水清又甜，
花朵红又香。

房子盖起来，
新房盖起九十间。
相好人儿住下来，
变成新村寨。

The bank did not move,

but the clear water did.

The bank and the water were separated.

The tree did not move,

but the leaves did.

The tree and the leaves were separated.

Zhugu Yulepai,

Whose tears were running like the water in the rivers.

Kaimei Jiuming Jin,

Who looked back three times at every step.

The young lovers were separated by

mountains and rivers, difficult to meet again.

Climbing over nine mountains,

they came to a new place.

After crossing seven rivers,

they found a good place.

The pasture on the hillside was flourishing.

The dam was wide.

The water in the river was clear and sweet.

The flowers were red and fragrant.

Houses were built,

ninety in number.

The young lovers settled down,

forming a new village.

田地开起来,
水渠理起来。
新渠理出十二条,
条条渠水灌田苗。

牧儿牧女成对对,
相好人儿成双双。
剩下开美久命金,
孤单好悲伤。
不见小哥羽勒排,
泪水汩汩淌。

松树配柏树,
白雪配白云,
黄金配宝石,
珊瑚配珍珠,
开美久命金,
要配羽勒排。

鸳鸯对对飞,
被狂风吹散。
情郎与情女,
被父母拆散。

除了小圆镜,
没人来照她,
除了银手镯,
没人来握她。

They cultivated the land.

They built canals.

Twelve new canals were built,

all to irrigate seedlings.

The young shepherds and shepherdesses were in pairs,

Lovers becoming couples.

But Kaimei Jiuming Jin was all by herself,

lonely and sad.

Not seeing Brother Yulepai,

she was in floods of tears.

Pine trees were a good match with cypresses.

White snow was a good match with white clouds.

Gold was a good match with gemstones.

Corals were a good match with pearls.

Jiuming Jin and Yulepai

were a match with each other.

Like the mandarin ducks in pairs

that were blown apart by fierce wind,

the young lovers

were torn apart by their parents.

Except for her small mirror,

no one was her companion.

Except for her silver bracelet,

no one was holding her hands.

不是没人来照她，
不是没人来握她，
百面镜子来照她，
千只热手伸向她，
开美久命金，
只是添烦恼。

圆镜明晃晃，
那代表羽勒排的心。
银镯热火火，
那代表羽勒排的意！

把玩小圆镜，
心头明亮亮。
抚摸银手镯，
心头暖洋洋。

风吹树叶沙沙响，
疑是羽勒排走来。
门外牧狗汪汪叫，
疑是羽勒排到来。

开美久命金，
等待又等待。
羽勒排哥哥，
一定会追来！
······

It was not that no one was accompanying her.

It was not that no one held her hands.

Hundreds of mirrors looked upon her.

Thousands of hands were extended to her.

But to Kaimei Jiuming Jin,

they only deepened her agony.

Her round mirror was bright,

as was the heart of Yulepai.

Her silver bracelet was warm,

as was the love of Yulepai!

Holding the little round mirror,

she felt her heart was brightened by it.

Touching the silver bracelet,

she felt her heart was warmed by it.

Leaves rustling in the wind,

she wondered if Yulepai had come.

Dogs barking outside the door,

she wondered if Yulepai had arrived.

Kaimei Jiuming Jin

waited and waited.

Brother Yulepai

would surely come for me!

...

孤雁穿云飞，
云遮雁不见。
朱古羽勒排，
心逐白云翔。

手摸刀鞘儿，
刀鞘嵌宝石，
宝石亮晶晶。
不是宝石亮晶晶，
那是久命的眼睛！

手摸刀把儿，
刀把镶珊瑚，
珊瑚明熠熠。
不是珊瑚明熠熠，
那是久命的眼睛！

朱古羽勒排，
看刀好心伤！
烤火火不暖，
煨茶茶不香。

白云如有脚，
请你站下来。
让我跨上去，
追逐到天边。

A single wild goose came flying through the clouds
but then disappeared behind them.
Zhugu Yulepai's heart
was flying with the white clouds.

He touched the sheath,
And the gems on the sheath,
Which were glittering.
They were not the gems glittering,
but the eyes of Jiuming!

He touched the handle of the sword,
And the coral on the handle,
Which was shining.
It was not the coral shining,
but the eyes of Jiuming!

Zhugu Yulepai
was so heart broken at the sight of the sword,
that he neither felt the warmth of the fire,
nor smelled the fragrance of the tea.

If clouds had feet,
please come down,
allowing me to get on you,
helping me follow her to the ends of the sky!

雄鹰冲天飞，
白鹿离窝逃。
朱古羽勒排，
要学白鹿一样逃。

初一晚上想要逃，
独角碗儿不会跑。
父母眼睛盯得牢，
这天晚上跑不了。

初二晚上想要跑，
两脚公鸡飞不高。
父母眼睛盯得牢，
这天晚上跑不了。

初三晚上想要逃，
铁三脚被塘火燎。
父母眼睛盯得牢，
这天晚上跑不了。

初四晚上想要逃，
四脚板凳钉得牢。
父母眼睛盯得紧，
这天晚上跑不了。

The mighty eagle soared into the sky.

The white deer abandoned the nests fleeing.

Zhugu Yulepai

wanted to run away just like they did.

He planned to flee on the first night of the month,

but like a one-legged bowl, he could not run.

Under the close watch of his parents' eyes,

he could not escape that night.

He planned to flee on the second night of the month,

but like a rooster with two feet,

he did not know how to fly high.

Under the close watch of his parents' eyes,

he could not escape that night.

He planned to flee on the third night of the month,

but he was like the iron-tripod with its feet burnt by the fire.

Under the close watch of his parents' eyes,

he could not escape that night.

He planned to flee on the fourth night of the month,

but the bench was nailed to the ground.

Under the close watch of his parents' eyes,

he could not escape that night.

初五晚上想要逃，
五间房门关得牢。
父母眼睛盯得紧，
这天晚上跑不了。

初六晚上想要逃，
六斗炒面还没炒。
父母眼睛盯得牢，
这天晚上跑不了。

初七晚上想要逃，
七星明亮天空照。
父母眼睛盯得牢，
这天晚上跑不了。

初八晚上想要逃，
八堆麦子还没打。
父母眼睛盯得牢，
这天晚上跑不了。

初九晚上想要逃，
九架犁牛没喂饱。
父母眼睛盯得牢，
这天晚上跑不了。

He planned to flee on the fifth night of the month,
but all the five doors were locked tight.
Under the close watch of his parents' eyes,
he could not escape that night.

He planned to flee on the sixth night of the month,
but he had not fried the six *dous* of noodles.
Under the close watch of his parents' eyes,
he could not escape that night.

He planned to flee on the seventh night of the month,
but the seven stars were shining bright in the sky.
Under the close watch of his parents' eyes,
he could not escape that night.

He planned to flee on the eighth night of the month,
but he had not threshed the eight piles of wheat.
Under the close watch of his parents' eyes,
he could not escape that night.

He planned to flee on the ninth night of the month,
but he had not fed all the nine farm cattle full.
Under the close watch of his parents' eyes,
he could not escape that night.

初十晚上想要逃,
十背柴火没砍好。
父母眼睛盯得牢,
这天晚上跑不了。

天天晚上想要逃,
日子天天择不好.
父母眼睛盯得牢,
天天晚上跑不了。

He planned to flee on the tenth night of the month,
but he had not chopped the ten piles of fire wood.
Under the close watch of his parents' eyes,
he could not escape that night.

He planned to flee every night,
but none of the dates was a good one.
Under the close watch of his parents' eyes,
he was not able to escape any night.

第五章　遭　　斥

开美久命金，
是个好姑娘。
手上戴银镯，
银镯叮当响。
头戴金耳环，
耳环亮闪闪。

久命心儿灵，
久命手儿巧。
久命织麻布，
会织十样花。
久命做活路，
会做百样活。

白云做经线，
白风做纬线，
白银做机架，
黄金做梳环，
宝石做梭子，
玛瑙做踏板。

Chapter 5　Being Wronged

Kaimei Jiuming Jin
was a good young lady.
On her wrist was a silver bracelet
that was jangling.
On her ears were gold earrings
that were glittering.

Jiuming was bright with her mind.
Jiuming was skilled with her hands.
She could weave flax linen
with ten different designs.
She could do handwork
that was hundreds in kind.

The white cloud was her warp;
The white wind, her weft;
the white silver, her rack;
the gold, her comb ring;
the gemstones, her shuttle; and
the agates, her pedal.

开美久命金，
织麻泪不干。
手丢宝石梭，
心想羽勒排。

泪水滴麻布，
麻布花点点。
血泪染麻布，
麻布红斑斑。

这天天晴且暖和，
久命坐在织机旁。
一只鹦鹉飞下来，
停在久命织机上。

久命求鹦鹉：
"背棵树去会很重，
带片树叶不会重。
背桶水去会很重，
带片水花不会重。

"带筐东西会很重，
带个口信不会重。
鹦哥呵鹦哥，
帮我带个口信吧！
三句知心话，
带给羽勒排。

Kaimei Jiuming Jin
had tears running nonstop as she wove,
gemstone shuttle in her hand
and Yulepai in her heart.

Tears dropped on the linen,
leaving flower-like blotches.
Tears with blood dyed the linen,
with red spots.

One sunny and warm day,
when Jiuming was sitting by the loom,
a parrot landed by her
and on her loom.

Jiuming begged the parrot for help:
"It would be very heavy to carry a tree,
but it would not be heavy to carry a leaf.
It would be very heavy to carry a bucket of water,
but it would not be heavy to carry a few drops of it.

"It would be very heavy to carry a basketful of things,
but it would not be heavy to carry a message.
Parrot, ah parrot,
please send a message for me!
I have a few heart felt words,
for Yulepai.

"高高天空中，
星斗亮闪闪。
孤星有三颗，
没有归星座，
一颗就是我。

"辽阔大地上，
青草密麻麻。
青草有三丛，
羊子没啃过，
一丛就是我。

"热闹村落里，
青年人很多。
姑娘有三个，
没跟男子亲近过，
一个就是我。

"快马加金鞍，
快来迎接我①。
带着百褶裙，
快来迎接我。
带着绕线架，
快来迎接我！"

---

① 接新娘是中国婚礼仪式中的传统习俗。通常在婚礼开始前，新郎要去新娘家请新娘出门，然后护送她参加婚礼，这就叫"接新娘"。在古老的纳西族习俗中，新郎去接新娘的时候，通常会送给新娘一些礼物，如裙子、绕线架等。

"High in the sky,
stars are sparkling.
But three lone stars
belong to no constellation,
and one of them is I.

"On the vast ground,
green grass is dense.
But three patches
have not been grazed by sheep,
and one of them is I.

"In the bustling village,
there are numerous young people.
But three ladies
have not been close with men,
and one of them is I.

"On a fast steed with a gold saddle,
you should hurry up to pick me up!①
With a skirt of a hundred pleats,
you should hurry up to pick me up!
With a reel for winding the yarn,
you should hurry up to pick me up!"

---

　　① Picking up the bride is a traditional custom in Chinese wedding ceremony. Usually, before the ceremony, the bridegroom goes to the bride's home to escort her to the wedding, and this is called "picking up the bride". In the ancient Naxi custom, when the bridegroom went to pick up the bride, as a tradition, he should send her some gifts, such as the skirt, the yarn reel, etc.

好心的鹦鹉，
不辞路迢迢。
久命的口信，
带到羽排家。

朱古羽勒排，
听了鹦鹉话，
眼泪哗哗淌，
心像锥子扎。

想对鹦鹉说实话，
父母不让说。
狠心的父母啊，
抢着来数落：

"高高天空中，
星斗亮闪闪。
星星归星座，
不会有孤星，
就虽有三颗，
颗颗不是她。

"星亮不久长，
一旦被云遮，
不会再发光。
那颗就是她。

The kind parrot,
not afraid of the long journey,
carried Jiuming's message
to Yupai's home.

Zhugu Yulepai,
on hearing the parrot's words,
had tears streaming down,
felt as if an awl was piercing his heart.

He wanted to tell the parrot the truth,
but his parents forbade him from doing so.
The cruel parents
began talking the moment the parrot finished.

"High in the sky,
stars are sparkling.
All belong to constellations,
with no exception.
Even if three stars were left out,
none of them would be she.

"The constellations do not stay the same for long.
Once covered by the clouds,
a star will sparkle no more.
That star is she.

"辽阔大地上，
青草密麻麻。
是草羊要啃，
不会有剩草。
就虽有三<u>丛</u>，
<u>丛丛</u>不是她。

"青草不长久，
<u>一旦</u>下白霜，
草就枯死了。
那<u>丛</u>就是她。

"热闹村落里，
青年人很多。
男女混一起，
准会起风波。

"她的怀中呀，
盘着小青蛇！
她的肚里呀，
蹲着小青蛙！
这样的姑娘，
怎能来我家！

"快马备金鞍，
不会去接她。
带着百褶裙，
不会去接她。

"Vast on the ground,
green grass is dense.
All grass will be grazed by sheep
with no grass that is not.
Even if three patches were left,
none of them would be she.

"The grass does not stay green forever.
Once white frost comes,
a patch of grass dies.
That patch is she.

"In the bustling village,
there are many young people.
Where there are men and women close together,
there are trouble and scandal.

"Clinging to her bosom
is another man.
Deep in her belly
is another man's baby!
How can a young woman like this
come to our home!

"On a fast steed with a gold saddle,
my son will not go fetch her.
With a skirt of a hundred pleats,
my son will not go fetch her.

带着绕线架，
不会去接她。

"好儿要配好姑娘，
我家儿子不配她。
好鞍要配好马上，
我家鞍子不配她。"

鹦鹉记性好，
句句记不漏。
飞回久命处，
句句说出来。

开美久命金，
只觉天旋地在摇。
眼泪落地地开裂，
久命的心开裂了。
太阳照着不温暖，
久命的心冰冻了。

"带去好心话，
招来恶意骂。
不好的名声，
背上一背脊。
九条河来洗，
不会洗白了。

With the reel for winding the yarn,
my son will not go fetch her.

"A good young man deserves a good young woman,
and she doesn't match our son.
A good saddle is for a good horse,
and she doesn't deserve our saddle."

The parrot had a good memory
and remembered every word.
On flying back to Jiuming,
it passed on the message word by word.

Kaimei Jiuming Jin
felt that the sky was spinning and the ground, shaking.
The ground cracked when her tears fell on it,
as was Jiuming's heart that was broken.
The sun was shining but was not warm to her,
because her heart was frozen.

"My heart felt message
brought me slanderous scolding.
The bad reputation
has become mine to carry.
Even if washed by nine rivers,
my innocence will not be restored."

"老虎爬高崖,
跌下高崖来。
黄猪滚泥塘,
难辨本来色。

"青藤绕青树,
树直才绕缠;
已经绕上了,
不能再解开。"

伤心坐树下,
树叶掉落了。
伤心坐河边,
河水干涸了。

青夜扪心坎,
身影多孤单。
难忍不白冤,
不如死了算!

抱个大石块,
走到大河边。
河水清又清,
身影映河里。

水花绿莹莹,
波光亮晶晶。
久命的眼睛呀,
明亮如水清。

"Like a tiger climbing the cliff,
once fallen,
it wallows in the mud like a yellow swine.
Its original color is hard to recognize.

"Lush vines can climb up the green tree,
only when the tree is straight.
But once the tree is covered with the vines,
it can't free itself from them."

So sad was she sitting under the tree,
till the leaves started to fall.
So sad was she sitting by the river,
till the rivers started to dry up.

How disappointed she was!
How lonely she felt!
Unable to bear the wrong that was impossible to redress,
she'd rather end her life!

Holding a big stone,
she walked to the riverside.
The water was clear and clean,
with her reflection in the river.

The splashes of the water were shiny green.
The choppy waves were shimmering bright.
Ah, Jiuming's eyes
were as bright as the clear water.

阿哥羽勒排，
爱过久命这双眼。
阿哥没叫久命死，
久命怎能投水死！

久命姑娘啊，
转到石岩边。
勾起心酸事，
直想跳下岩。

太阳照高崖，
崖壁白生生。
久命脸庞呀，
也是白生生。

阿哥羽勒排，
爱过久命这张脸。
阿哥没叫久命死，
久命怎能跳崖死！

久命姑娘啊，
手拿黑毛绳。
来到松树下，
心酸想上吊。

雨雪洗松树，
松叶青油油。
久命的发辫呀，
也是青油油。

Brother Yulepai
loved Jiuming's eyes.
Without Yulepai's permission,
how could Jiuming drown herself!

Ah, young Jiuming
walked to the edge of a cliff.
Reminded of her grief,
she only wanted to jump.

The sun was shining on the cliff,
blanching the cliff wall.
Ah, Jiuming's face
was as pale as the cliff wall.

Brother Yulepai
loved this face.
Without his permission,
how could she jumped to her death!

Ah, young Jiuming,
with a black coarse rope in her hands,
came under a pine tree.
Grief-stricken, she wanted to hang herself.

Washed by the rain and snow,
the pine leaves were shiny green.
Ah, Jiuming's braided hair
was also shiny green.

阿哥羽勒排，
爱过久命好发辫。
阿哥没叫久命死，
久命怎能去吊死！

Brother Yulepai

loved Jiuming's braided hair.

Without his permission,

how could she hang herself!

第六章　盼　　望

青青的竹林，
被高山遮住。
两眼望穿了，
不见心上人。

茂盛的花草，
被高崖隔住。
嗓子喊哑了，
喊不来情人。

泪水滴麻布，
麻布白花花。
血泪染麻布，
麻布红彤彤。

织机声声哀，
姑娘哭断肠。
泪眼望天空，
鹦鹉又飞来。

Chapter 6　Waiting

The green bamboo forest
was shrouded by the shadows of the high mountains.
Jiuming had worn out her eyes looking,
but there was no sight of her sweetheart.

Lush flowers and grass
were separated by high cliffs.
She had called till her voice was hoarse,
but there was no trace of her sweetheart.

Tears dropped on the linen,
staining the white linen with tear blotches.
Tears with blood dyed the linen,
dyeing the linen pinkish red.

Every sound of the loom was sad.
The young woman cried till her heart was broken.
Looking at the sky with her tearful eyes,
she saw the parrot had come again.

"好心的鹦鹉，
请你停一停！
前久托你带的话，
怕没替我全说到？
你不是露中鹤，
怕在云中失落了，
你不是山中虎，
怕在山里失落了。

"好心的鹦鹉，
多带东西会很重，
带个口信不会重。
请你再带三句话，
告诉阿哥羽勒排。

"白鹿喝过山泉水，
泉水甜味会在心。
羊儿嚼过青青草，
青草香味会在心。
你和我的事，
难道不在心？

"不是银子呀，
配不上金子。
不是珍珠呀，
配不上宝石。
不是羽勒排，
配不上久命。

"Kind-hearted parrot,

please stop for a minute!

The message I asked you to send,

did you send all of it?

I was wondering,

Since you are not a crane,

could the message be lost in the clouds?

And since you are not a tiger,

could the message be lost in the mountains?

"Kind-hearted parrot,

it would be very heavy to carry many things,

but it would not be heavy to carry a message.

Please bring a few more words

to Brother Yulepai.

"Having drunk from the mountain spring,

the white deer would keep the sweetness in its heart.

Having chewed on the green grass,

the sheep would keep the fragrance of the grass in its heart.

The love between you and me,

isn't it in your heart?

"If it is not silver,

it does not match gold.

If it is not pearl,

it does not match gem.

If he is not Yulepai,

he does not match Jiuming.

"快马备金鞍，
快来接我吧。
带着百褶裙，
快来接我吧。
带着绕线架，
快来接我吧！"

好心的鹦鹉，
找到羽勒排。
久命说的话，
照样说一遍。

朱古羽勒排，
听完心已碎。
恳求鹦鹉鸟，
回信给久命：

"白鹿饮泉水，
甜味在心里。
羊儿吃青草，
香味在心里。
妹的知心话，
深记我心里。

"冬天要来接。
冬天三个月，
大雪纷纷下。
山谷积满雪，

"On a fast steed with a gold saddle,
come fetch me!
With a skirt of a hundred pleats,
come fetch me!
With a reel for winding the yarn,
come fetch me!"

The kind-hearted parrot
found Yulepai
and repeated exact words,
as Jiuming had said.

Zhugu Yulepai
was heartbroken on hearing the message.
He begged the parrot
to take his message back to Jiuming:

"Having drunk from the mountain spring,
the white deer does keep the sweetness in its heart.
Having chewed on the green grass,
the sheep does keep the fragrance of the grass in its heart.
Your loving words
are engraved deeply in my heart.

"I tried to come to fetch you in winter,
but in the three months of winter,
it snowed continually.
Valleys were covered with deep snow,

109

道路被雪封。
父母眼睛比雪冷，
要走走不成。

"春天要来接。
春天三个月，
青草刚发绿，
庄稼还未熟。
青黄不接啊，
父母不给我出门，
要来来不成。

"夏天要来接。
夏天三个月，
天天下暴雨，
洪水流满地。
父母心比洪水狠，
要走走不成。

"秋天要来接。
秋天三个月，
三月九十天，
放羊九十天。
父母跟在我后边，
要来没法来。

"我的有情小妹呵，
请你再等三五天，

and roads were blocked by heavy snow.
With my parents' eyes colder than the snow,
I couldn't escape as I would like.

"I tried to come to fetch you in spring,
but in the three months of spring,
the green grass was just sprouting,
and the new crops hadn't come in.
As it was a period of food shortage,
my parents forbade me from going out,
so I couldn't come to you as I would like.

"I tried to come to fetch you in summer,
but in the three months of summer,
it poured day after day.
The flood water was flowing everywhere.
My parents are crueler than the floods,
so I couldn't leave for you as I would like.

"I tried to come to fetch you in autumn,
but in the three months of autumn,
I had to herd the sheep
on all the ninety days of the three months.
My parents were following me wherever I went,
so I couldn't find a way to come as I would like.

"My dear little sweetheart,
please wait for a few more days.

阿哥就要来接你，
阿哥就要来看你。"

开美久命金，
白天望白云，
晚上望星星，
唯愿白云带他来，
唯愿星星带他来。

想着这时要来了，
这时不见来。
想着这天要来了，
这天不见来。
想着这月要来了，
这月不见来。

白天听见马铃响，
想是羽排来接她，
丢下织梭迎出去，
却是别人骑着马。

夜里门儿响，
想是羽排来敲门，
急忙披衣迎出去，
哪知是风在打门。

I am coming to fetch you.
I am coming to see you."

Kaimei Jiuming Jin,
gazing at the white clouds during the day,
gazing at the stars at night,
only wished that the white clouds would bring him along,
only wished that the stars would bring him along.

She thought he would have come by now,
but he had not.
She thought he would have come by this day,
but he had not.
She thought he would have come by this month,
but he had not.

Hearing the horse bell ringing during the day,
she thought it must be Yupai who came to fetch her.
putting down the shuttle, she ran out,
only to find another man riding the horse.

Hearing the sound of the door at night,
she thought it must be Yupai knocking on the door.
Quickly putting on her coat, she rushed out,
only to realize it was the wind blowing at the door.

久命盼呵盼，
脖子望酸了。
久命等啊等，
眼窝盼凹了。

小哥羽勒排，
莫非是个负心人？
久命失望了，
心里好悲凄！

一阵清风徐徐吹，
歌声进耳里。
那是游主①的声音，
那是爱神在劝慰。

"久命姑娘呵，
快把眼泪揩掉吧，
快来巫鲁游翠阁②。

——————————

① 游主：纳西族神话传说中的爱神。掌管着年轻人的殉情行为。
在纳西族历史上，青年男女为爱而献身的现象已经成为纳西族文化的
一部分，因而丽江古城也被誉为"殉情之都"。
② 巫鲁游翠阁：纳西族传说中情侣们幸福生活的理想之地。据
东巴经典籍记载，巫鲁游翠阁是人们相亲相爱、永葆青春的神奇圣地。
"巫鲁"的意思是玉龙雪山。"阁"指山上草深林密的地方。

Jiuming yearned for him so hard
that she strained her neck.
Jiuming awaited him for so long,
that her eye sockets were sunken.

Brother Yulepai,
could he have betrayed me?
Jiuming was disappointed.
How saddened she was!

A gentle and cool breeze blew,
bringing her the singing voice.
It was the voice of Deity You①.
It was consolation from the god of love.

"Ah, Young lady Jiuming,
wipe off your tears quickly!
Come to the holy land of Wuluyoucuige②!

---

① Deity You is the god of love in the Naxi legend, who manages the
youth's dying for love. In the Naxi history, the phenomenon that the young
men and women gave their life for the sake of love has become a part of its
culture. That is why the city of Lijiang is called "the capital of dying for
love".

② The holy land of Wuluyoucuige: In the Naxi legend, the holy land
of Wuluyoucuige is the ideal place for lovers to live a happy life. According to
records in the Dongba classics, the holy land of Wuluyoucuige is a magic and
sacred place where people love each other and stay young forever. "Wulu"
means the Yulong snow mountain. "Ge" refers to the place on the mountain
where the grass is deep and the forest is thick.

115

你的两眼呀，
来看美丽的鲜花。
你的双脚呀，
来踏柔软的草滩。
你的双手呀，
来挤白鹿的鲜奶。

"久命姑娘呵，
快把眼泪揩干吧，
使者就要来接你。
树上蜂蜜任你采，
高山清泉任你饮，
金花银花任你戴……"

久命听歌声，
眼前生幻景。
白鹤来迎接，
白鹇来迎接，
蜻蜓来迎接，
蝴蝶来迎接……

开美久命金，
一条麻索腕上挂，

With your eyes,

come to look at the beautiful flowers.

With your feet,

come to walk on the tender grassland.

With your hands,

come to milk white deer.

"Ah, young lady Jiuming,

quickly wipe off your tears,

For the messenger is coming to fetch you soon.

You will be free to gather honey on any tree,

to drink from any spring in the mountains, and

to wear any gold or silver flowers."

As Jiuming listened to the song,

her mind's eye saw

the white crane that came to fetch her,

the silver pheasant that came to fetch her,

the dragonfly that came to fetch her,

And the butterfly that came to fetch her.

Kaimei Jiuming Jin,

with a linen rope around her wrist,

走上十二道岩子坡①，
来到黄香木树下。

"黄香树啊黄香树，
请你收留我，
细麻索啊细麻索，
请你同情我。"

好心的鹦鹉，
飞去又飞来。
只见织机空荡荡，
不见久命织绸麻。
羽勒排的贴心话，
不知向谁传。

---

　　① 十二道岩子坡：纳西族民俗中的殉情圣地，在很多东巴经典
籍中均有记录。据记载，十二道岩子坡是圣地"巫鲁游翠阁"的一部
分，而另一部分叫"游翠鲁美拿"，意即"情死者（之地）的大黑
石"，乃"巫鲁游翠阁"与外界的交界之处；二者合在一起，便是完
整的"巫鲁游翠阁"。据记载，十二道岩子坡是玉龙雪山下的一片草
甸。

walked to the Twelfth Cliff Slope①,
and came under the Yellow Fragrant Tree:

"Yellow Fragrant tree,
please take me in!
Ah, the thin linen rope,
please be merciful with me."

The kind-hearted parrot
looked here and there,
only to find the empty loom
with no Jiuming weaving.
Yulepai's caring words,
to whom should they be taken?

---

① The Twelfth Cliff Slope is the shrine for the Naxi people who choose to die for love. In the vast Dongba classics, it is recorded that the Twelfth Cliff Slope is part of the holy land of "Wuluyoucuige", whereas the other part is "Youcuilumeina", which means "the big black stone where lovers die for love and where 'Wuluyoucuige' is connected to the outside world". According to records, the Twelfth Cliff Slope is a meadow under the Yulong snow mountain.

第七章　双　　殉

羽排想久命，
日里夜里想。
乱麻塞心间，
吃饭饭哽喉，
喝茶茶也呛。

劈柴斧不快，
放羊鞭不响。
羊群乱哄哄，
一时都跑散。

天黑才回家，
父母又来骂：
"一头黄牯牛，
今天走丢了。
丢牛不去找，
牧神要责罚。
赶快点火把，
连夜把牛找！"

Chapter 7　Meeting Again

Yulepai missed Jiuming

day and night,

troubled and restless.

He could not help choking on his food when eating,

and he could not avoid coughing when dinking tea.

When chopping the firewood, he found his axe dull.

When herding the sheep, he couldn't crack his whip.

His flock was noisy and disorderly,

running in all directions.

When he finally got home after it was dark,

he was faced with his parents' scolding:

"A yellow bull

was lost today.

If we don't look for it,

we will be punished by the god of animal husbandry.

Light a torch quickly,

and go find it tonight!"

朱古羽勒排，
就像脱牢笼。
丢了黄牯牛，
他没记心窝。
只想找久命，
心里急似火。
翻山又越岭，
脚步快如风。

跨过七条谷，
翻过九座山，
爬上十二岩子坡，
来到黄香木树前。

只觉天昏昏，
只觉地暗暗，
朱古羽勒排，
晕倒在地上。

久命有灵魂，
发出哀怨声：
"我托鹦鹉鸟，
带去口信一百次。

"又托鹡鸰鸟，
带去口信一千回。
朱古羽勒排，
你也太狠心！"

Zhugu Yulepai

ran like he had just escaped from a cage.

The loss of the yellow bull

could not be farther away from his mind.

Finding Jiuming was the only thing

that was burning on his mind.

Crossing mountains and hills,

his feet were moving like wind blowing.

After seven valleys

and nine mountains,

he went up to the Twelfth Cliff Slope

and stood in front of the Yellow Fragrance Tree.

Feeling that the sky was gloomy

and the earth, murky,

Zhugu Yulepai

passed out on the ground.

The soul of Jiuming

uttered grievance in a mournful voice:

"I asked the parrot

to send the message a hundred times.

"And I asked the wagtail,

a thousand times.

Zhugu Yulepai,

you are too cruel!"

朱古羽勒排，
伤心又难过：
"久命姑娘呵，
你带口信一百次，
你捎口信一千遭，
次次带到我家了。

"白羊吃过嫩青草，
香味长存在嘴里，
白鹿喝过甜泉水，
甜味还留喉咙里。

"你的三句知心话，
像墨滴在清水里，
化在我的心坎上，
溶在我的血液里。

"头回要想捎口信，
父母抢着诅骂你，
句句话呀像毒刺，
戳在你心上，
痛在我心里。

"二次我托鹦鹉鸟，
给你传回音。
我的口信呵，
可曾捎到你那里？

Zhugu Yulepai

felt forlorn and wretched:

"Ah, dear Jiuming,

Your one hundred messages and

one thousand messages

were all sent to our house.

"Having had the tender green grass,

the white sheep has the fragrance in its mouth for a long

time.

Having just drunk from the sweet spring,

the white deer could still taste the sweetness in its throat."

"Your heart felt words,

like drops of ink falling into the clear water,

have been kept in my mind

and engraved in my heart.

"The first time I wanted to send you a message,

father and mother would have nothing but defaming you.

Each word was like a poisonous splinter,

poking your heart,

And paining mine."

"The second time I asked the parrot

to send a message to you.

ah, my message,

did it reach you?

我的三句话，
鹦鹉可曾告诉你？

"喂好肥猪已三年，
窖酒①备下已三年，
只盼春暖花儿开，
去接如花好姑娘。
哪知美丽金银花，
早已凋谢了。
我的久命呵，
像花一样凋谢了！"

开美久命金，
魂儿来说话：
"怕是鹦鹉来迟了，
怕是小妹走早了，
两两相错了，
你的口信没接到。

"我曾盼你又怨你，
我曾爱你又恨你，
如今是非明白了，
后悔却已迟。"

---

① 窖酒：一种传统的丽江酒，香醇甘甜，深受纳西族人民的喜
爱。它之所以被称为窖酒，是因为它的酿造必须在一个密封的酒窖中
进行。

And my words,

did the parrot pass them on to you?

"I have raised fat pigs for three years.

I have saved up wine in the cellar① for three years.

I was only waiting for the blooming spring days,

when I could come to fetch you, pretty as a flower.

Never did it occur to me that the gorgeous honeysuckle

had withered away.

Ah, my dear Jiuming

had withered away like a flower!"

The soul of Kaimei Jiuming Jin replied:

"I'm afraid the parrot must have come too late

or I must have left too early.

We missed each other,

and your message I did not get.

"I used to pine for you but blame you at the same time,

I used to love you but hate you at the same time.

Now I know and I regret,

although it is too late."

---

① Cellar wine is a traditional Lijiang wine, mellow and sweet, popular among the Naxi people. It is called cellar wine because its brewing process has to be conducted in a sealed cellar.

"小哥羽勒排，
不要难过了。
我还活着时，
不能成一双。
如今我已死，
不能再成双。

"这棵大树下，
埋有我的金和银，
埋有我的好珠宝，
就作礼物留给你，
你快取出回家吧！"

朱古羽勒排，
眼泪如喷泉。
"金银我不要，
珠宝我不拿，
久命姑娘呵，
只要跟你在一块。

"花朵凋谢了，
来年还会开。
久命姑娘啊，
能像花朵重开吗？

"Brother Yulepai,

don't be sad!

When I was alive,

we couldn't be a couple.

Now that I am dead,

we can no longer become one.

"Under this big tree

were buried my gold and silver

and my fine jewelry.

Let them be the gifts I have left for you.

Find them quickly and bring them home with you."

Zhugu Yulepai,

Cried with tears poured out like water coming from a spring:

"Gold and silver I don't want.

Jewelry I won't take.

Ah, dear Jiuming,

I only want to be with you.

"Withered flowers

will bloom in the coming year.

Ah, dear Jiuming,

will you bloom again like the flower?

"给你安上珠宝眼，
还能看见吗？
给你镶上金银牙，
还能吃饭吗？
给你绸裳氆氇褂，
还能穿戴吗？
给你接上山羊气，
给你接上绵羊气，
还能说话吗？
把你接到我家里，
接到我的内房里，
还能谈笑吗？"

"射出去的箭，
不能回头了。
泼下地的水，
舀不回来了。

"阿哥羽勒排，
我只求你一件事。
把我烧成白骨灰，
把我烧成青烟尘，
让我洁白的灵魂，
随白云一起飘行！"

"花朵凋落了，
绿叶跟着落。
泉水干涸了，
鱼儿不独活。"

"If the jewels could be your eyes,
will you be able to see again?
If gold and silver could be your teeth,
will you be able to eat again?
If silk and wool could be made into gowns,
will you be able to wear them again?
If the breath of the goats
and the sheep could be yours,
will you be able to breathe again?
If I could take you home with me,
and sit you down in our room,
will you be able to talk and laugh again?"

"The arrow that is already shot out
can't return.
The water that is already splashed out
can't be ladled back.

"Brother Yulepai,
I beg of you for only one thing:
Let me become white ashes and
celestial blue-colored dust.
Let my pure soul
fly with the white cloud!"

"When flowers have withered,
green leaves follow along.
When spring water has dried up,
fishes do not live by themselves."

131

"小妹久命请等等，
等我跟你来。
两个知心合意人，
永远不分开！"

羽排脱下白披毡，
轻轻盖在久命上。
拢来松枝和柏叶，
放在她周围。

一团烈火熊熊燃，
羽排跳进烈火里。
浓烟滚滚漫天卷，
化作白云冲天起。

十二道岩子坡，
烈焰照天红。
两朵白云多美丽，
飞腾追逐在蓝空。

"Little Sister Jiuming Jin, please wait,
wait for me to join you.
Two intimate lovers
will never be apart again!"

Taking off his white coat,
Yupai gently covered Jiuming with it.
Collecting pine branches and cypress leaves,
he put them around her.

When the fire was blazing,
Yupai leaped into it.
The dense smoke rolled up and
became white clouds rocketing into the sky.

On the Twelfth Cliff Slope,
the roaring flames illuminated the sky.
Lovely were the two white clouds,
flying and chasing in the blue sky.